the tiniest sound

by Mel Evans

with watercolors by Ed Young

Doubleday & Company, Inc.
Garden City, New York

For Emmy and Tom—
my own special two.

My mother once told me that
the tiniest sound in the world
is a shadow
just my size
and just my shape
that jumps into bed with me
and pulls my blanket
up and up—and up
until there is no shadow
at all.
Silently
he goes out with the light,
to wait for me
until tomorrow.

CAN YOU THINK OF A TINIER SOUND?

Maybe
the tiniest sound in the world
is the moonbeam
that slides down our roof,
slips between the leaves of the tree
outside my window,
creeps across the window sill
and fills the toes of the slippers
beside my bed.

COULD THERE BE A TINIER SOUND THAN THAT?

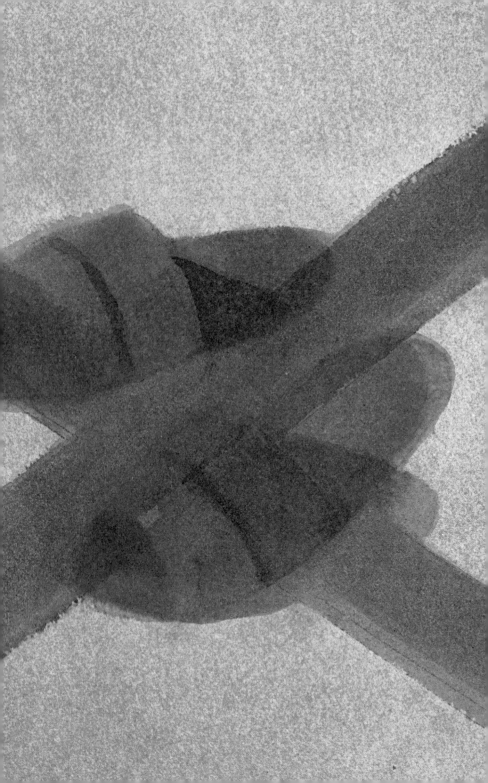

Some people say
the tiniest sound in the world
is the first little drop of water
that gathers itself
from the mist on my window,
and while I watch,
slides slowly down the pane—
first this way and then that way—
until, running fast as it grows,
it slants across the glass
and makes a little pool
where the window ends.

ISN'T THAT THE TINIEST SOUND IN THE WORLD?

My friend says
the tiniest sound in the world
is the fog
that comes in over the river,
covers the tops of the tallest buildings,
then slips down to cover
the water towers,
and the chimneys,

and while I watch
pushes against my window
until it makes
all the street lights
look like
furry blurs.

WHAT SOUND COULD BE TINIER THAN THAT?

When it is autumn,
the tall grass on the hill
below our house
turns yellow and red and purple
and all the other colors.
Sometimes the wind blows,
and the speckled leaves
sprinkle down into the grass
and then—
the whole hill
moves in running waves
like the ocean.
I can hear the wind...
But the waves
break silently.

WOULD THERE BE A WHISPER IF YOU WERE THERE?

I have heard it said that
no sound could be smaller than
the flight of a gossamer milkweed seed
caught in a warm summer breeze,
carried beyond the top of the trees,

across the pasture,
and gently set
on the soft white coat
of a spring-born lamb.

COULD YOU HEAR THAT?

A very young friend
once told me that
the tiniest sounds
were the nighttime footsteps
of the littlest kitten
walking across the furry rug
to sit by the fireplace
and warm herself
by silent red coals.

WHAT IS SOFTER THAN KITTEN PAWS ON FUR?

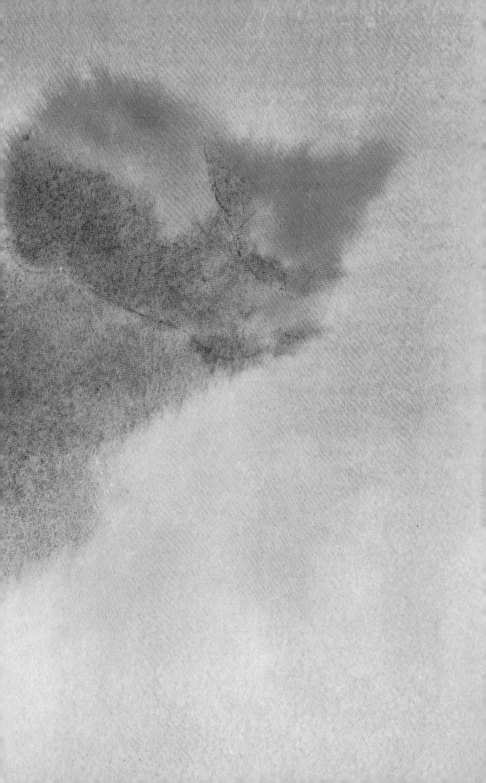

I used to think
the tiniest sound in the world
might be a baby snowflake
leaving a little white cloud
to drift gently down
through a misty sky

to the softest spot
on the tip-top tassel
of a snuggly cap
on the snoozely head
of a furry
baby
bunny.

WHAT DO YOU THINK…?

I have heard that
the tiniest sound in the world
is the first crocus
sending a thin green leaf
through a sun-made spot
beside a snowdrift
outside my window.
And before I am awake
it drops spots
of green
and red
and yellow
on the white glitter
that was winter.

CAN YOU DREAM OF SUCH A TINY SOUND?

At our house
there is a busy brook
that rushes down to the river.

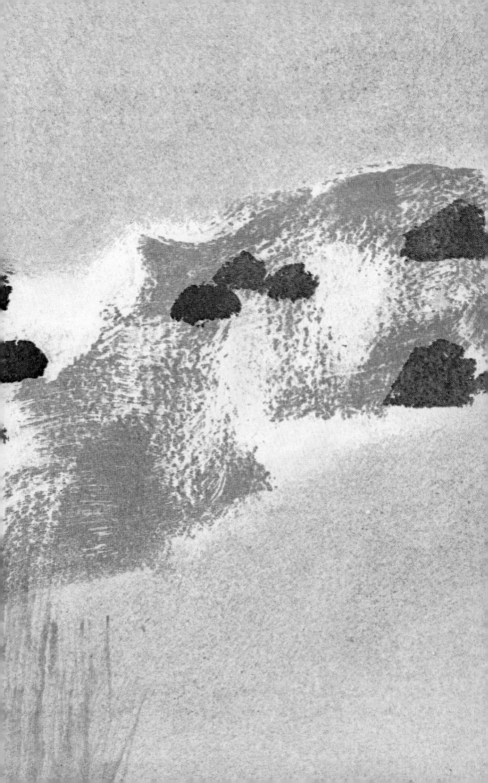

But sometimes, behind green rocks,
it rests in deep, quiet pools.
And there, where all is still,
silver-sided little fish
come to rest from noisy water
and in the shadows
of dark brown twigs
lie napping.

DO YOU THINK YOU COULD HEAR THEM?

Remember the quiet that
comes after the summer shower.
The wind that roared through the oaks
and then sighed sadly
in the hemlock hedge
ripples the lake
and is gone.
Now, a mischievous breeze,
stirred by new sunlight,
rustles the glitter-wet leaves
of our smallest aspen tree.

COULD YOU REALLY HEAR THAT?

Sometimes I think that
the tiniest sound
I have ever heard
are the footsteps of the spotted fawn
who drinks at sunrise from our pond,
walks most delicately
on pointed feet
into the greening garden
to nibble the smallest lettuce leaf,
and then moves silently as a shadow
into the leaf-speckled shade
of the orchard
as she goes.

COULD ANY SOUND BE MORE DAINTY?

Still...
The tiniest sound in the world
may be a baby hummingbird
tiptoeing past his sleepy mother
to the edge of the nest
to try his silky wings
before he flies silently down
to sip honey water
from a flower
dipped in glistening dew.

CAN YOU THINK OF A TINIER SOUND?

Most people say that
the looping inchworm
who measures our fresh-white fence
makes no sound at all.
But I think he does.
He scrunches up—like this...
And then he reaches—like that...
To catch the tiny twig
That sways across his way.
He walks on many little toes,
but I am sure he makes
at least a tiptoe sound.

COULD ANYTHING ELSE BE SO STILL?

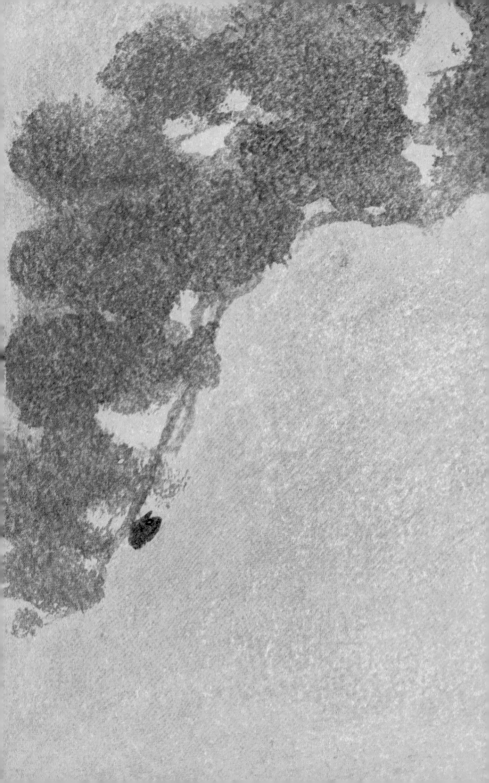

It could be that
the very tiniest sound
is heard only at sunset,
when the youngest butterfly
who has fluttered day-long
From red flower...
To white...
To yellow...
Sits on a cozy twig,
folds his wings,
and yawns.

HOW DOES A SLEEPY BUTTERFLY YAWN?

A little girl once told me that
the tiniest sound in the world
is the squeak of the red balloon
she bought from the man in the park
and led by the string
until it flew away
over the trees,

above the pigeons,
up beside the tall building
and around the water tower
until it became
a spot...

And then a dot
in the sky
that she couldn't see
at all
any more.

IS A BALLOON IN THE SKY THE TINIEST SOUND?

MEL EVANS has been in the book business for thirty years. He has been an editor of fiction, non-fiction, and children's books. He is now retired and lives in Ridgefield, Connecticut, with his wife.

ED YOUNG was born in China. He received most of his education in America and attended art school in California and New York. He is an American citizen and lives in New York where he works as a free-lance artist and also teaches at Pratt.

He was runner-up for the Caldecott award in 1967 for his illustrations for *The Emperor and the Kite*.